# The Three Little Pigs

## A Tale about Working Hard

*Retold by Julie Hawksley and Sharon Yates*
*Illustrated by Colin Petty*

Famous Fables™

Reader's Digest Young Families

Once upon a time, there were three little pigs who lived together with their aunt in a little cottage at the edge of the forest. She was a loving aunt and had sewn each little pig his own colorful coat with big shiny buttons.

Each little pig slept in his own little bed, and each had his own little bucket for food. But as the three little pigs grew bigger, the cottage seemed to get a little smaller.

So one fine day, the three little pigs set out to build their own houses.

The first little pig decided to build his house next to a stream. He liked the idea of living close to the water. This way he wouldn't have to walk through the forest to the stream and then all the way back again. He could play in the water whenever he wanted.

After the first little pig picked the spot for his house, he saw that all the other animals were playing in the sun. "It's much too nice to work all day," he said. So he built his house very quickly out of bundles of straw and rope. Then the first little pig skipped off to splash in the stream.

The second little pig wandered farther along the road. Then he stopped and sat down under a big shady tree.

"It's far too hot to work," said the second little pig. So he decided to take a little nap instead. When he awoke, he gathered some sticks and built his house in no time at all.

Then he sat down again under the shade of the big tree and watched the bees as they buzzed from flower to flower.

Now the third little pig also wandered down the road. He saw the other animals playing. He felt hot from the sun. As he walked, he remembered hearing about a big bad wolf who lived in the forest.

"I better build a strong house," he said. "I will build my house out of bricks. I don't want the big bad wolf catching me!"

The third little pig worked hard on his house all day. He didn't stop to play or to take a nap until his house was finished. Then he joined the other two little pigs, who were playing.

In a short while, it began to grow dark. The birds flew to their nests, and the rabbits hopped into their burrows. The bees flew back to their hive. The third little pig noticed that all the animals were going to their homes. He decided to go into his house to be safe.

"He is being silly," said the other two pigs. "There is still time to play." They started to sing and dance a jig.

At that moment, the big bad wolf jumped out from behind the trees.

"Help!" the two little pigs cried, and they ran to their houses as fast as they could. They reached their homes just in time and locked the doors.

The big bad wolf raced up the path to the first little pig's door.

"Let me in," the big bad wolf growled in a loud voice outside the house made of straw and rope.

"No! No!" cried the first little pig. "Not by the hair of my chinny chin chin." And the little pig jumped onto his bed and hid under the quilt.

"Then I'll huff and I'll puff and I'll blow your house down," cried the big bad wolf. And so he did.

Then the first little pig jumped out of his bed and ran as fast as he could to the house of sticks built by the second little pig. He dashed inside the house just in time and locked the door!

"Let me in," growled the big bad wolf in his loud voice.

The two little pigs huddled together in fear.

"No! No!" they each cried. "Not by the hair of my chinny chin chin." And the two little pigs hid under the table.

"Then I'll huff and I'll puff, and I'll blow your house down," cried the big bad wolf. And so he did.

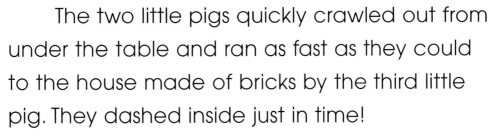

The two little pigs quickly crawled out from under the table and ran as fast as they could to the house made of bricks by the third little pig. They dashed inside just in time!

"Let me in," growled the big bad wolf in his loud voice.

"No! No!" cried the three little pigs. "Not by the hair of my chinny chin chin."

"Then I'll huff and I'll puff, and I'll blow your house down," cried the big bad wolf. The big bad wolf huffed and he puffed, and he puffed and he huffed, but he couldn't blow down the little brick house!

By now the big bad wolf was out of breath!

"All right," he called to the pigs. "I'll climb down the chimney!"

The first two little pigs hid in the cupboard, but the third little pig went to the fireplace, where there was a small fire. He fanned the flames to make them higher.

"Yeeow!" yelled the wolf as the flames scorched his tail. The big bad wolf jumped out of the chimney and ran away. He was never seen again, and the three little pigs lived happily ever after.

# Famous Fables, Lasting Virtues
# Tips for Parents

*Now that you've read* The Three Little Pigs, *use these pages as a guide to teach your child the virtues in the story. By talking about the story and its message and engaging in the suggested activities, you can help your child develop good judgment and a strong moral character.*

## About Working Hard

Young children are naturally like the first two little pigs in the story—they usually choose a path that is the easiest and quickest way to having fun. But children are often willing to delay their desire for immediate gratification in order to please you. You can build upon this desire to help your child develop the virtues of self-discipline, resourcefulness, and working hard.

1. *Establish a routine.* Doing chores helps to teach your child responsibility and self-discipline. By helping to make your household run smoothly, your child will feel that what she does is important and, by extension, that she is important. Make it clear to your child that you expect the chores to be completed in a timely fashion. If you say you will impose consequences for undone chores, you need to follow through. Otherwise your child learns you don't really mean what you say.

2. *Demonstrate hard work.* Call your child's attention to how much work was involved in developing a skill you or your spouse have, whether it be a sport, a household skill, a hobby, or a job-related skill. Many young children are unaware of the time and effort it takes to become adept at something. They often feel frustration at not being able to perform at a level they expect—especially when they are learning to do something new.

3. *Better to show than to tell.* If you leave dirty coffee cups around or forget to make your bed, it's hardly fair to expect your children to clear their places and make their beds. If you pick up after yourself, your children are much more likely to follow your example.